Nana's Garden

By Jenelle Zingg and Tim & Oliver Fleming

Illustrated by Ros Webb

Copyright © by Jenelle Zingg and Tim Fleming.

All rights reserved.

This book or any portion thereof may not be reproduced or used in any manner whatsoever without the express written permission of the publisher except for the use of brief quotations in a book review.
Printed in the United States of America 2020.

It is with admiration and appreciation that we dedicate this book to Nana. There is much talk in the world today about needing a village to raise a child. Nana is our village. She is right next door and spends time each week teaching Oliver about numbers, letters, and how to hold a pencil. More importantly, however, she offers her insight about what it means to be kind, compassionate, thoughtful, and a good friend. We feel so grateful for Nana's support on this journey through parenthood. Ruthness is the hero in the book, and you are our hero.

We love you, Nana.

"Here, girls," Oliver whistled, blocking the path of a white chicken with one black feather as she tried to escape behind the feeding bucket. "Not that way, this way, up this ramp!"

Nana picked up her basket and laughed, "You look like you're herding cats!"

"I am. Well, I'm herding chickens. I'm training them," explained Oliver as he chased around the new chickens. "Our older chickens just sit there and our new group keeps running away from me."

"I can't imagine why," grinned Nana.

"I'm going to be the best chicken trainer ever," Oliver continued.

"Well, Oliver, if you want them to come to you, you will have to be patient and work hard to make them more people-friendly," smiled Nana.

"Nelly, Fluffy II, and Rubia (the older chickens) along with Marble, Edith, and Patches (the newer chickens) are doing well. But this white chicken has attitude!" said Oliver, pointing to the white chicken with the black feather. Oliver thought for a minute.

"Nana, you're a good teacher!" Oliver jumped up suddenly. "You've taught me lots of things. Like working with clay, growing the garden, and how to make pesto from our basil plants. Maybe you can help me train the chickens, Nana!"

"Well, we can try," said Nana, taking off her gardening gloves and putting her hand to her chin. "We are going to need lots of patience and, of course, some chicken treats (birdseed)."

"How hard can that be?" said Oliver in a funny voice. Just as he said it, the white and black chicken made a break for it around the water bowl. Oliver and Nana laughed.

"Even the very best chicken trainers need to stop for a snack break," said Nana when they had caught their breath.

Oliver, Nana, and Deedah sat in the sunshine, enjoying a nice glass of lemonade. They watched as the birds flitted around the birdfeeder in the backyard and jockeyed for position to get the best food.

The cool lemonade was just what they all needed after a hard morning's work. Nana had been busy weeding the vegetable beds. Deedah had been clipping and shredding branches to make mulch.

"What are you up to this afternoon, Ollie?" smiled Deedah. "Do you want to help me plant some tomato seeds in the greenhouse?"

"Yes. How do we do that?" Oliver asked. Deedah showed Oliver how to plant the seeds in little containers and then water the plants so they will grow. Once they were done with the seeds, Deedah said, "These plants are ready to be transplanted into the garden. Oliver, grab your shovel."

Deedah and Oliver went to plant the new seedlings in the garden soil. "There, these will do well here," Deedah said.

"Be sure to put away your shovel when you are done using it, Oliver," reminded Deedah. Ollie gave Deedah a bit of an eye roll before jumping up and running to the greenhouse to hang his shovel on the hook.

After helping Deedah, Oliver went back to training his chickens into the late afternoon. Oliver found it hard to be patient, but easy to give out chicken snacks, and, on occasion, he couldn't help but to run after the chickens.

"I think I'll give the chickens a rest," said Oliver. "I don't want to tire them out."

"That's a good idea," said Nana. "They need their rest if we want them to lay eggs for us. Why don't you let the chickens rest until tomorrow, and we can pick some blackberries? The chickens should have some beautiful fresh eggs for us by the morning, and we can make German pancakes or Dutch babies for breakfast."

"Yes!" cried Oliver, "I'll go get the blackberry bowl."

Oliver rushed into the house. His muddy boots came flying out the door behind him as he kicked them off.

Oliver and Nana filled not one, not two, but three whole bowls with blackberries.

"I can't believe how many there are," sighed Oliver.

"Shall I tell you the secret?" said Nana, winking. "It's Deedah's magic mulch. It traps all the moisture and goodness in the soil, helping the blackberries grow strong and sweet."

Oliver ran his hands through the fine tree clippings and let it trickle back down. The clippings felt rough and had a sweet, woody smell.

Before long, it was time for Oliver to walk back to his house.

"I'll just go say goodnight to the chickens," he said.
"Good night, Rubia, good night, Fluffy II, good night PatchyPoo, good night Edith, good night, Marble, good night Nelly. "And good night to you too," Oliver said to the white chicken with the one black feather.

Oliver was still deciding on a name for her. He wanted to choose a name that matched her personality.

"Good night, my sweet boy," said Nana, giving Oliver a huge hug, "I'll see you first thing in the morning for blackberry pancakes!"

Oliver went through the fence back home to where his Mama and Papa were waiting for him.

The next morning, Oliver sprung out of bed, raced downstairs and out the door to Nana's. He was still wearing his pajamas.

"Oliver, please get dressed before you go outside," said Mama.

"And brush your teeth!" said Papa.

"Sorry, Mama and Papa, no time!" cried Oliver, "I've got to go and see if there are any eggs."

"Well, at least put on some shoes!" said Mama. "And grab your hat," said Papa, as they both laughed out loud. Oliver screeched on his brakes and reversed back into the house, beeping like a truck. He put on his muddy boots, grabbed his hat and roared off again through the fence to Nana's.

When Oliver reached the chicken pen, something didn't look right. The door to the coop was open, and there were feathers on the ground.

"This is very suspicious," thought Oliver.

He stepped slowly, careful not to disturb anything. He was just like a detective in one of the stories Nana told him as they worked in the garden.

The three older chickens and Nelly were all huddled up in the corner of the coop and the three others were missing. There were no eggs. Not a single one.

"Maybe they didn't lay any because all the training had tired them out?" thought Oliver.

"Or maybe..." Oliver quickly counted the chickens. One, two, three, four. Where was Marble, Edith, and the white chicken with the black feather?

Just then, Nana came out of her house.

"Nana, Nana, the new chickens are gone!" cried Oliver. "Do you think they ran away?"

Nana surveyed the scene and found Marble in her pottery studio at the edge of the garden. "I don't think so, Ollie," said Nana sadly. "Let's look at the clues. Marble flew the out of the coop, Edith and the white and black chicken are still missing and there are feathers all around."

"And there are no eggs," said Oliver. Then he spotted a bit of broken eggshell in the straw.

"And there are only white feathers. Look, they are all over" said Oliver. "Edith has black and brown feathers so those feathers are not hers."

"Go get your Papa so he can help us look for Edith," Nana directed. Oliver did as he was told and came running back with his Papa.

Both Oliver and Papa searched the garden and then over the back fence and found Edith hiding in the bushes. Papa climbed over the fence and brought back one very scared chicken.

"Look here, Oliver," pointed Nana. "There are tracks in the mud."

"Those are weasel tracks!" cried Oliver.

"I'm afraid you're right," said Nana. "A weasel must have gotten in and taken the eggs, scared Edith and Marble out of the pen and taken the white chicken."

"It looks like she put up a good fight," said Oliver, pointing to the feathers.

"She probably protected the other chickens from being eaten," Papa said.

As the three of them searched the chicken coup, Nana found the body of the half-eaten chicken. Oliver sadly asked, "Is the white and black chicken dead now, Nana?"

"I'm afraid she is," said Nana. "The weasel would have eaten what it needed and left."

Nana put her arm around Oliver with Oliver holding his papa's hand, and they stood quietly for a moment.

"Ruthness. I'm going to call her Ruthness," said Oliver at last. "Because she ruthlessly gave her life defending the other chickens."

"That is a very good name. Ruthness will be remembered as a hero," said Nana.

Oliver's Papa got a shovel from the toolshed, dug a big hole in the chicken run and they buried Ruthness where she likely stood guard, protecting the other chickens.

"What will happen to Ruthness now, Nana?"

"Well, everything in nature is connected. You know that the butterflies come lay their eggs on the milkweed we plant, so their caterpillars can eat. And we turn the tree clippings into mulch to help the blackberries grow. Well, the weasel needed to eat, so it took our chicken. But I believe the connection carries on even after things die, so Ruthness might come back in her next life; she might be another chicken or a butterfly."

"Or even a weasel?" asked Oliver.

"Maybe. But I hope not!" said Nana. "We don't want to lose any more chickens."

"I'm going to make a picture of Ruthness, so we can always remember her and how brave she was. Ruthness the Hero," said Oliver.

"That's a lovely idea," said Nana. "And while you're doing that, I'll whip us all up a treat. We might not have any eggs, but we sure have plenty of blackberries!"

"Enough for a blackberry crumble?" asked Oliver.

"Enough for ten blackberry crumbles!" laughed Nana.

"That's alright then, but we only need one," he said, giving Nana a great big hug.

Made in the USA
Middletown, DE
10 December 2022